FOR ANDREW

Buck Wilder

Publisher's Cataloging-in-Publication Data
Author: Smith, Timothy R.
    Buck Wilder's Little Skipper Boating Guide: a complete introduction to the world of boating for little skippers of all ages/by Timothy R. Smith, author and Thomas G. Mills, illustrator - Traverse City, Michigan:
    Alexander & Smith Publishing©, 2001
    p: 64 col. ill.; 28cm.

    ISBN: 0-9643793-6-8
    UPC: 7-53240-79368-2

    SUMMARY: A complete introduction to the world of boating for children.
    1. Boating for children. I. Title. II. Little skipper boating guide.

Illustrator: Thomas G. Mills

GV777.56 .S55 2001   00-092806
797 . 1/083--dc21   CIP

10 9 8 7 6 5 4 3 2 1 - First Edition

Printed in China

Buck Wilder© books are available for bulk purchase.
For details contact:
Buck Wilder Adventures
4160 M-72 East
Williamsburg, MI 49690
(231) 938-3009 or 1-800-994-BUCK
Fax (231) 938-3263
www.buckwilder.com

I love to go boating. When I'm on the water I feel connected to all around me. It doesn't matter what kind of boat I'm in, I just love being on the water. This is a boating guide meant to help all you "little skippers" of all ages enjoy the wonderful world of boating.

 *First* - Many thanks to all those that contributed and helped to put this book together. It was the combined energy and talents of many people - far too many to mention, and to the end, Buck Wilder will always be thankful.

 Second - Thanks for reading this book. I hope you enjoy it, have fun with it, and learn from it!

 *Third* - Please remember this is a guide and not the gospel of boating. It is written for the pure enjoyment of being on the water and appreciating all that surrounds us and how we are connected to it.

Finally - I'd like to send a special thanks to those people who take the time in their lives to help others. You know who they are…those individuals and organizations who help us with boating safety, good manners, and respect for the water and nature that surrounds us.

Buck Wilder

It is my hope that you will enjoy the pages of this book because I enjoyed putting them together for you. They are fun, interesting, and I hope very informative for all you "little skippers". Enjoy the great world of boating that we all share, use this as a guide, and always respect the water you're on.

CONTENTS

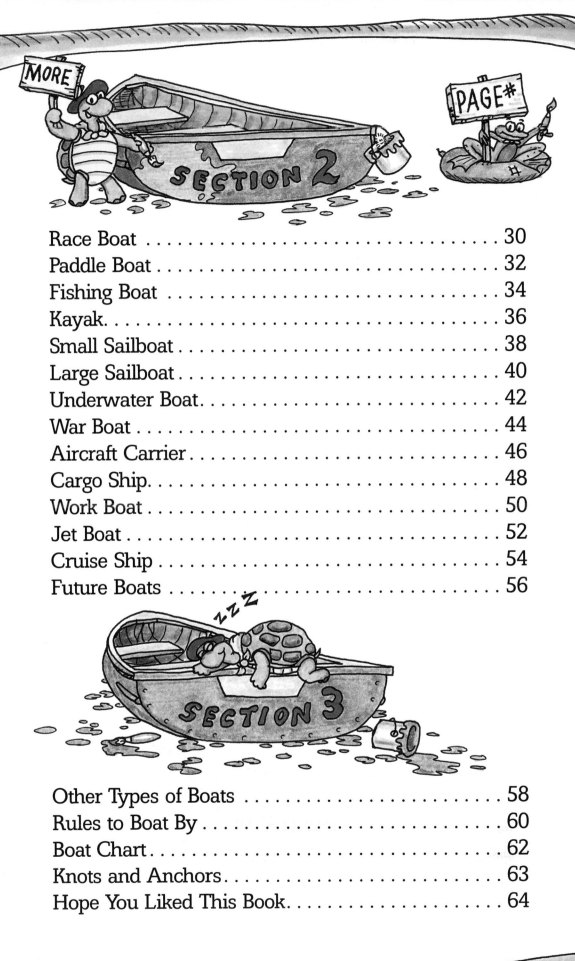

If you think about the pure basics of a boat you'll realize boats are made to float on water and get you and your cargo from one point to another. The size, style, and use of the boat depend on what you are trying to accomplish. Most often, one boat will not serve all purposes and that is why we have so many different kinds of boats.

HISTORY of BOATING

Boats came before all forms of travel. Mankind has always wanted to know what was on the other side and boats got us there. Our earth is 2/3rds covered with water so we basically have always and will always need boats. Studying our fascinating history of boating will give a better understanding of our present world of boating and the future to come.

LEWIS & CLARK

STEAM BOAT

DELTA QUEEN

MOBY DICK

S. S. MINNOW

GILLIGAN'S ISLAND

PEARL HARBOR

US

PETER PAN AND CAPTAIN HOOK

MUTINY ON THE BOUNTY

CAPTIAN NEMO AND THE NAUTILUS

AMERICA'S CUP

TREASURE ISLAND

How does steel float? What keeps thousands of pounds from not sinking into the water? The answers have to deal with physics and density. Very simply, if the ship and its cargo weigh more than the water the ship displaces, the ship will sink! That is why you can not overload a boat or ship… because down it will go! Therefore, the ship and its cargo must always weigh less than the water it displaces. This principle applies to all boats. Pay attention to safety and never overload a boat with extra people or cargo.

There is a basic design to every boat, no matter the size. The most important is, it has to float and be able to carry some added weight. Most boats need a front (or bow) that will cut through the water and not plow it or push it. The middle section needs to be flat or wide enough not to cause the boat to roll or tip over. It also must be designed deep enough to hold the weight you want to carry.

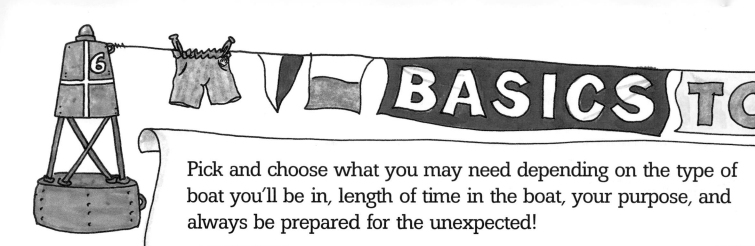

BASICS TO

Pick and choose what you may need depending on the type of boat you'll be in, length of time in the boat, your purpose, and always be prepared for the unexpected!

THE VERY BASICS

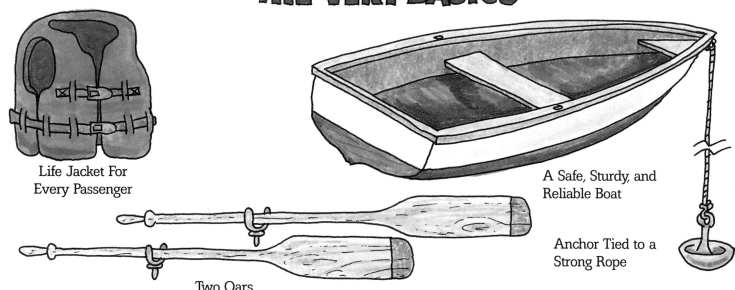

Life Jacket For
Every Passenger

A Safe, Sturdy, and
Reliable Boat

Anchor Tied to a
Strong Rope

Two Oars

EXTRA

(FUN T

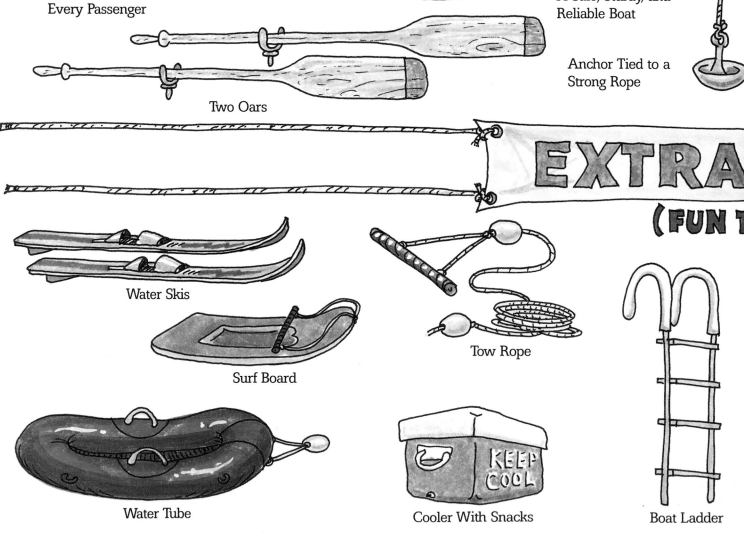

Water Skis

Surf Board

Tow Rope

Water Tube

Cooler With Snacks

Boat Ladder

GET STARTED

RECOMMENDED TO HAVE
(To Be Prepared For The Unexpected)

Floating Seat Cushion

Extra Rope

Extra Lifesaving Equipment

Sunscreen

Flashlight

Extra Paddle

First Aid Kit

Compass

Horn

Extra Clothing

Something To Bail Water

Pocket Knife

EMERGENCY PACK

May contain a whistle, extra batteries, sunglasses, hat, insect repellent, money...

STUFF
(HAVE)

BAIT

Fishing Equipment

TACKLE BOX

Swim Trunks

A Big Flashlight

Buck's Fishing Book

Portable Toilet

All Kinds of Water Toys

Camera

19

A basic Row boat is the easiest and the best boat to start out with. I recommend everyone take the time in their life to sit in a small boat with two oars and practice rowing, turning, and backing up. It is not only fun but it will build great confidence.

An Inboard has a propeller and a driveshaft connected to a motor contained inside the boat. Usually the motor (similar to a car engine) is covered up and unseen. Most inboards, including the classic older wooden ones, have fairly large engines with a lot of power. Inboards built today come in a large variety of sizes, shapes, and colors.

Race boats are to other boats like race cars are to other cars. They are built sleek, powerful, and made to go real fast. Being a race boat driver is just like being a race car driver except you are in a boat and on the water. Some race boats have been known to travel at speeds in excess of 200 mph. If the boat had wings, it would fly!

A Typical Paddle Wheel

As the wheel turns it pushes the water backwards moving the boat forward - or the same principle in reverse.

The old Mississippi paddlewheelers conjure up feelings of Huckleberry Finn, Tom Sawyer, and rafting away down a sleepy river. Today, paddlewheelers come in all sizes and shapes and still work on the same "paddle wheel" system. Connected blades rotate through the water either pushing or pulling the craft it belongs to. Small paddleboats are like pedaling a bike but only on the water.

I CAN'T BEAR IT!

BEAR BACK

BEAR VALANCH!

JER-"BEAR?"

SOMETHING IS FISHY HERE!

ROCK OF AGES

I OTTERLY LOVE THIS PLACE!

Kayaking can be very quiet and peaceful...or rip-roaring, if you want it to be. Either way, you'll paddle along in harmony with the nature that surrounds you. In the ultimate test, kayaks will take you places that no other boats can. Once you learn the skill of balance and paddling you'll skim across the surface like you belong there.

Small sailboats are usually single masted and hold one or two people. They work on the simple system of catching the wind and sailing toward your destination. Once you learn how to "tack into the wind" a whole new world of sailing adventures will open up to you. Learn how to handle this size boat before you move onto the big stuff.

Large sailboats come in all sizes, shapes, and colors. They have carried pilgrims, pirates, cannons, cargo, and almost everything imaginable for thousands of years. As expected, they are exciting and thrilling to be on. You can still travel the earth in them, sleep in them, and even live in them. They work just like a small sailboat - just larger.

WAR boats have a fascinating history. The very first carried spears, bows, and arrows. Next came wooden ships with cannon balls, then steel ships with long range cannons and guns, and then came missiles and rockets... all with the intent to fight and defend. It is interesting to read about the armadas that sailed our oceans, the pirates that stole from them, and the secrets the sea never tells.

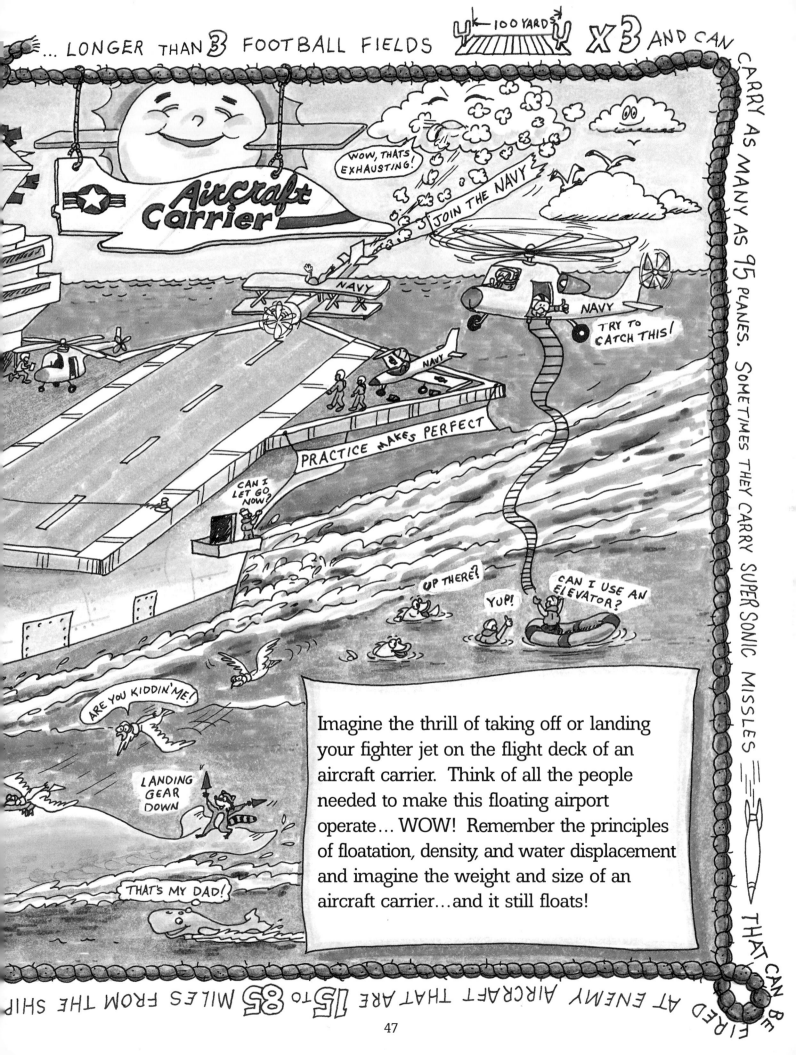

Imagine the thrill of taking off or landing your fighter jet on the flight deck of an aircraft carrier. Think of all the people needed to make this floating airport operate... WOW! Remember the principles of floatation, density, and water displacement and imagine the weight and size of an aircraft carrier...and it still floats!

Our earth is more than 2/3rds covered with water so we need all kinds, types, and sizes of cargo ships. Iron ore, corn, cars, toys, food, and almost everything imaginable is carried from one point to another by cargo ships. These ships are either <u>Liners</u>, which operate on a regular schedule, or <u>Tramps</u>, which take goods where and when they are needed. Cargo ships have rules of travel just like cars or airplanes.

A Typical Work Boat

There are as many different types of work boats in this world as there are people that work on them. Their work is not always fun and can often be very strenuous or even dangerous. Those that work on the water are extremely aware of their surroundings, paying close attention to changing weather conditions and the water that surrounds them.

Jet boats come in all sizes and shapes and run by jet propulsion. They are fast, versatile, and lots of fun to be on. Jet skis (small individual jet boats) turn quickly, are somewhat easy to handle and can give quite a thrill when scooting across the top of the water. They also can be very dangerous if you do not respect their speed and size. Always watch out for swimmers and travel way off shore.

Cross Section of a Typical Cruise Ship.

Most cruise ships come with swimming pools, sun decks, libraries, movie theaters, more food than you can eat, and lots of lounge chairs. They are like floating cities. Many people consider cruise ships to be the ultimate in vacation relaxation and travel. They offer everyone the opportunity to experience the high seas in ultimate comfort.

OTHER TYPES OF BOATS

There are so many different types of boats that it is almost impossible to list them all…but still fun to think about! Here are some examples of "other types of boats".

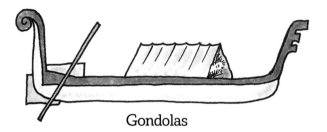

Gondolas

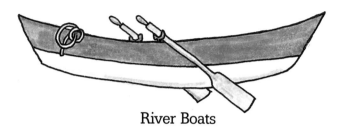

River Boats

Surf Boats

Ferries

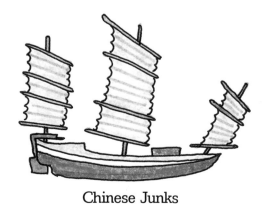

Chinese Junks

Tug Boats

Coast Guard

Amphicars

Ice Breakers

House Boats

Air Boats

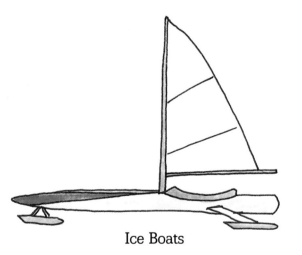

Ice Boats

Barges

Glass Bottom Boats

1 Everyone Wear a PFD.
(personal floatation device)

2 Know Your Boat.

3 Have a Float Plan.

FLOAT PLAN
✔ Tell Someone
✔ Tell Someone
✔ Tell Someone

- where are you going
- when you expect to get back
- who your passengers are

4 Check The Weather.

5 Bring The Equipment You Need.

6 Be Prepared For The Unexpected.

FIRE EXTINGUISHER
FLASHLIGHT
DISTRESS FLAG

TOOLS
EMERGENCY EQUIPMENT
FIRST AID

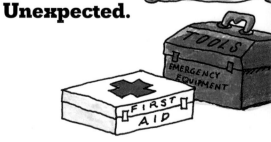

7 Take a Boaters Safety Class.

8 Know The Rules Of The Water.

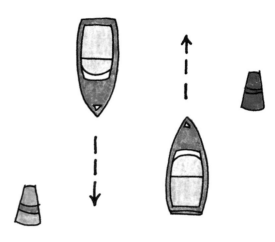

9 Be Courteous and Helpful.

KEEP A DISTANCE

10 Respect Your Environment.

11 Don't Ever Overload a Boat.

OOPS!

HONEY HO

DOWN LOAD

12 Learn How To Swim...

it's Fun!

BOAT CHART

Canoe

Row Boat

Small Outboard Motor

Large Outboard Motor

Inboard

Race Boat

Paddle Boat

Fishing Boat

Kayak

Small Sailboat

Large Sailboat

Underwater Boat

War Boat

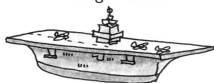
Aircraft Carrier

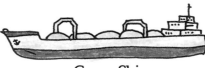
Cargo Ship

Work Boat

Jet Boat

Cruise Ship

Future Boats

Tie it up in knots

A Very Useful Loop Knot

BOWLINE

A Quick and Easy Knot

SQUARE KNOT

Will Tie and Untie Easily

SHEET BEND

Actually Used by Surgeons

 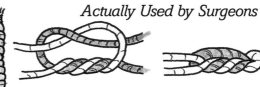

SURGEON'S KNOT

Good For Joining Two Lines

DOUBLE FISHERMAN'S

Very Strong and Secure

CONSTRICTOR KNOT

Can Be Tied With One Hand

CLOVE HITCH

Two Half Hitches Work Best

HALF HITCH

And Anchors

YACHTSMAN'S
ANCHOR

STOCKLESS
ANCHOR

MUSHROOM
ANCHOR

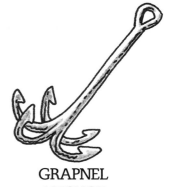

GRAPNEL
ANCHOR

63

I *really* hope you liked this book! I enjoyed putting it together for you. I've also written the _Small Fry Fishing Guide_ and _Small Twig Hiking & Camping Guide_…and have plans to write even more! So, keep in touch -

Thanks,

Buck Wilder